Usborne
10 More Ten-Minute Stories

Usborne
10 More
Ten-Minute
Stories

Designed by Laura Nelson

CONTENTS

JACK AND THE BEANSTALK

Jack and his mother lived all alone in a little cottage in a valley ringed by mountains. They were poor; so poor, their cupboards were bare and they had no money to buy food.

"We'll starve soon," said Jack's mother. "And we have nothing left to sell... except the cow. You'll have to take Milky White to market, Jack, and mind you get the best price you can for her."

Jack tied a rope around the cow's neck and led her away.

He hadn't gone far when he met an old man with bright eyes and a bushy beard.

"Stop there, boy," said the old man. "I'll give you five magic beans for your cow."

"Oh no," said Jack. "Mother wants me to sell her at the market. We need money, not beans."

"Aha!" said the old man. "But who knows what these beans will bring? They're magic, you know. They could bring you fortune, adventure, *treasure...*"

Jack's eyes grew round in wonder. "It's a deal!" he cried. He handed over Milky White, snatched up the beans and raced home, proud with what he had done.

Goodbye, old man!

When he showed his mother the beans, she was horrified. "I wanted gold coins, not old beans," she fumed. "Jack! Jack! What were you thinking? How are we going to buy food now?"

"But they're *magic* beans," said Jack. "At least, the old man said they were magic..."

How could you!

"You've been tricked, you fool," said his mother.
And she took the bag and threw it out of
the window, beans and all.

That night, Jack went to bed on an empty, grumbling stomach.

"I've ruined everything," he sighed. "Milky White is gone, so we don't even have any milk, and all I got for her were some rotten beans. How was I foolish enough to believe that old man? There's no such thing as magic!"

But the next morning, Jack opened his window to see... a twisting, turning, living, *magical* beanstalk!

"The beans *were* magic, after all!" cried Jack.
Looking up, he could see the beanstalk spiral its
way above the clouds.

And he coudn't resist... Here was
an adventure before his very eyes.
He reached out, grabbed hold of
a branch, and began
to climb.

Up, up, up he went, until his cottage was no more than a tiny dot in the distance. He climbed past soaring birds and through the airy blue until he reached the topmost tip of the beanstalk. And there, at the beanstalk's end, stood a castle in the clouds. And on the doorstep of that castle, a giantess.

"What have we here?" asked the giantess, picking up Jack as if he were no heavier than a feather. "A little human boy, I see," she said, her eyes as large and round as twin moons. "Well, it's not safe for you here. My husband has a taste for human flesh. He'll munch you and crunch you in a moment, a little scrap of a thing like you."

"Oh please," said Jack. "I'm so very, very hungry, and I won't be any trouble. Couldn't you give me just the tiniest of snacks and then I'll be gone, I promise. I haven't had a meal for days, and I've climbed all this way."

"Very well," said the giantess. "But whatever you do, don't you let my husband catch you."

And she carried him through to the kitchen.

Mmm! How delicious!

Jack feasted on bread crumbs bigger than his body and mounds of cheese as high as houses. He was just congratulating himself on his adventure when, all of a sudden... THUMP! THUMP! THUMP! The castle walls trembled and a great booming voice thundered down the hallway.

FEE, FI, FO, FUM!
I smell the blood of an Englishman.
Be he alive or be he dead,
I'll grind his bones to make my bread!

"Quick!" gasped the giantess. "That's my husband come back for his lunch. Hide in here," she whispered, dropping Jack into a sugar jar. "And not a peep or a squeak out of you!"

The giant sniffed the air. "What's this I smell? Is it BOY?"

"Oh no," said his wife. "No boys here. If you smell anything at all, it must be the remains of that boy you had for breakfast."

"Humph!" said the giant. "Then bring me my lunch! I'm hungry enough to eat a horse."

His wife hurried away and returned with a tray. All this time, Jack stayed as still as he could in the sugar jar, hardly daring to breathe.

After the giant had gobbled his lunch, he sat back in his chair and called out, "Wife! Bring me my hen! The one that lays the golden eggs."

His wife brought him the hen and, this time, curiosity got the better of Jack. He lifted up the lid and peered out of the jar. Sure enough, there was a hen and PLOP! out came a *real* golden egg.

The giant sighed with satisfaction then sank back into his chair once more. Soon he was fast asleep, with snores that shook the castle walls.

"Now's your chance," said the giant's wife, scooping Jack out of the sugar jar. "Be off with you my dear, and if you value your life, don't you *ever* come back again."

Jack took off like a spring hare. In one bound, he was down from the table and across the floor. But then he thought of his poor mother, cold and hungry at home, and of that fat, clucking hen, laying eggs of pure gold, and he couldn't resist.

He turned, picked up the hen and made a dash for the door.

"Squawk!" cried the hen. "Squawk! Squawk!"

The giant woke. "What's going on?" he cried.

"Hey!" he added, spotting Jack beetling across the floor. "There *is* a BOY, and he's stealing my hen. How DARE he! I'm going to catch him and gobble him up. Come back, boy! Come back now!"

Jack didn't stop, not for a second. He sped down the beanstalk, his feet fumbling for their holds, slipping and sliding down the treacherous trunk. And above him came the giant, making the beanstalk bend and sway.

"Mother!" called Jack. "Bring the axes. Please! Bring the axes."

His only hope was to make it down before the giant...

Hurry, Jack!

"I'll get you yet, BOY!" yelled the giant, making a grab for Jack.

But Jack twisted from his grasp. He tumbled down the last part and landed in a heap on the ground, still clutching the squawking hen.

"We've got to chop down the beanstalk!" cried Jack. "Before the giant makes it down."

Jack and his mother hacked away as hard as they could. And with each swift, hard stroke, the blades of the axes bit through the beanstalk, making it wobble, first this way, then that.

"Stop that!" boomed the giant. "Stop that, I say!"

With one final stroke, Jack sliced through the stalk. The giant yelled as he fell through the air. Down, down, down he came, hitting the ground with such force, Jack knew he would never be troubling them again.

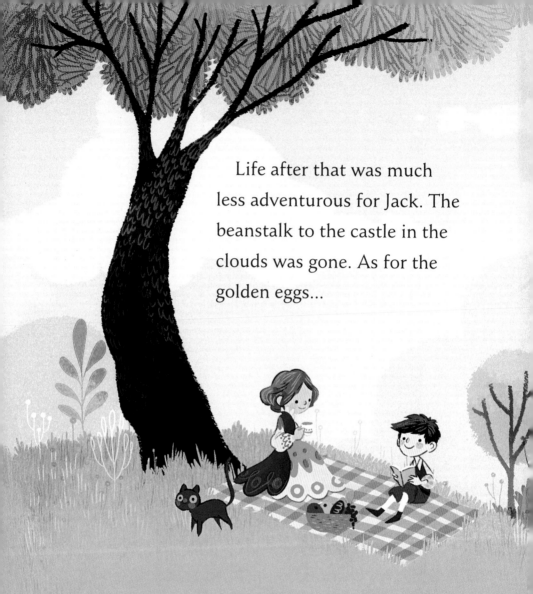

Life after that was much
less adventurous for Jack. The
beanstalk to the castle in the
clouds was gone. As for the
golden eggs...

...they bought Jack and his mother a new home
and food enough to last a lifetime.

But, sometimes, he couldn't help wishing for just one more magic bean...

THE GINGERBREAD MAN

Once upon a time there was a little old woman and a little old man who lived very happily together on their farm. They had everything they could want – a home, enough food to eat and money to spend, and a life they loved.

Every morning, the little old woman would rise early and milk their cow, so they had fresh milk for breakfast. The little old man would feed the horses and collect fresh eggs from their hens. Then they would sweep the farmyard so it was spick and span.

"I have just one wish," sighed the little old woman. "More than anything, I wish we had a child of our own."

One day, the little old woman decided to see if she could make one. So she opened her recipe book...

She measured and she mixed, she poured and she stirred until she had made her dough. Then she rolled it and shaped it and cut out a little man. He had three raisin buttons and a smiling face.

"There," she said. "Now we'll have a boy of
our very own."

And she put him in the oven to bake.

Soon, delicious gingerbread smells wafted
through the kitchen.

"Are you sure this will work?" asked the little old man. "Don't you think we might be too old?"

"Of course we're not too old," said the little old woman. "I'm sure he won't be any trouble at all."

And she went over to the oven door...

Meow!

No sooner had she
opened it than the
Gingerbread Man
leaped out of the oven
and began running at
top speed across the
kitchen floor.

He didn't stop
to say 'Hello' or
'Thank you' or 'How
do you do?' Instead
he shot straight out
of the open door.

"Oh!" cried the
little old woman.

"Come back! Come back!"
But the Gingerbread Man didn't stop. Instead
he sped on, a gleeful smile on his little
round face. And as he ran,
he chanted...

"Run, run, as fast
as you can, you can't
catch me, I'm the
Gingerbread Man!"

He ran past a horse and a cow.

"Come back!" they cried. "We want to eat you!"

But the Gingerbread Man laughed and said, "I've run away from a little old woman and a little old man and I can run away from you too, yes I can!"

Hee hee!

"Run, run, as fast as you can, you can't catch me, I'm the Gingerbread Man!"

And the Gingerbread Man sped on, with the little old woman, the little old man and the horse and the cow all chasing after him.

Stop!

The Gingerbread Man ran past a farmer in a field. "Stop!" cried the farmer. "I want to eat you!"

But the Gingerbread Man laughed and said, "I've run away from a little old woman, a little old man, a horse and a cow, and I can run away from you too, yes I can!"

Yum!

"Run, run, as fast as you can, you can't catch me, I'm the Gingerbread Man!"

"Stop! Stop!" everyone cried. But the Gingerbread Man sped on with the little old woman, the little old man, the horse, the cow and the farmer all chasing after him.

Soon, the Gingerbread Man came to a
playground full of children.

"Stop!" cried the children. "We want to eat you!"

But the Gingerbread Man laughed and said, "I've
run away from a little old woman, a little old man,
a horse, a cow *and* a farmer, and I can run away
from you too, yes I can!"

"Run, run, as fast as you can, you can't catch me, I'm the Gingerbread Man!"

And on he raced, with the little old woman, the little old man, the horse, the cow, the farmer and the school children all running after him.

Stop!
Stop!

But then he came
to a wide, wide river.
The Gingerbread Man
stopped. He couldn't
swim! And he could hear
everyone coming down
the hill behind him.

"Hello," said a sly
voice. The Gingerbread
Man turned. There
stood a fox.

"I can take you
across the river," said
the fox.

"Why don't you
climb on my tail?"
The Gingerbread
Man climbed onto
the fox's tail.

"Come back!" cried
the little old woman.
"Come back," cried
the little old man.
But the Gingerbread
Man just laughed.

"Run, run, as fast as you can," he sang. "You can't catch me, I'm the Gingerbread Man."

The fox went a little further across the river and then he said, "My tail is dragging in the water...

I would hate for you to get wet. Why don't you climb on to my back?"

So the Gingerbread Man climbed up the tail...

...onto the fox's back.

The fox swam even further across the river. "Oh dear," he sighed. "The water is going over my back now. Why don't you climb onto my head?"

It's a trick!

Stop!

So the Gingerbread
Man climbed onto the
fox's head.

"You'll be safe there," said the
fox, with a wink. "The water won't get you. Now,
are you ready?" he asked.

"Am I ready?" asked the Gingerbread Man.

SNAP!

"Ready for what?"

"Ready for this," said the fox. He tossed his head and the Gingerbread Man flew up, up into the air. The fox waited, his jaws open, his white teeth shining and then SNAP!

"Oh no!" cried the Gingerbread Man. "I'm a quarter gone."

The fox tossed his head again and SNAP!
"Oh no!" cried the Gingerbread Man. "I'm
half gone."

And SNAP!

"Oh!" cried the Gingerbread Man. "I'm three quarters gone."

And then SNAP! That was the end of the Gingerbread Man.

SNAP!

THE EMPEROR'S NEW CLOTHES

Long ago there lived an Emperor who loved, above all else, to dress in beautiful clothes. He had a coat for every hour of the day, different shoes for every dance and an outfit for every occasion.

When his soldiers came to tell him of their battles he would say, "Go away! I'm very busy deciding what to wear."

Do you like mauve?

When his ministers came to find him he refused to discuss important matters of state. Instead he asked them what they thought of his shirt.

Best of all, the Emperor loved riding around his kingdom showing off his new clothes for everyone to see. He would smile as the people exclaimed, "There goes the Emperor. He looks so fine!"

His finest clothes, he saved for the Royal
Procession. Only this year...

"I have nothing to wear!" wailed the Emperor.
"None of my clothes are good enough. I need a
NEW outfit and I need one NOW."

It has to be
spectacular!

"You there!" he shouted at his servant. "Find me an outfit. I need a new one immediately, do you hear?"

"What about the pink fur hat with the yellow feather?" suggested his servant. "Or the green velvet with gold cuffs?"

"Not good enough," stormed the Emperor. "What I need are the best clothes-makers in THE WORLD."

The Emperor's
servant set off at
once... but although
he found plenty of
tailors, none of them
would do.

Wanted:
Finest
tailors
in town

"Oh dear," said the servant. "I need the very,
very best, or the Emperor is going to be furious."
But then...

...two men rushed up to him.

"We are Slimus and Slick at your service. Take us to the Emperor at once!"

I'm Slimus.

I'm Slick.

They hurried through the streets to the palace, where the tailors bowed low before the Emperor.

"We make ingenious clothes," said Slick.

"Only clever people can see them," added
Slimus. "To foolish people, they are absolutely
invisible."

"That sounds perfect!" said the Emperor.
"Get weaving at once."

"First," said Slimus, "we need sacks and sacks of money, the best apartment in the palace and *absolute* privacy. We work alone."

That should do it!

After the Emperor had gone, the two tricksters laughed until their bellies ached and their faces turned purple.

"We did it!" they cried. "We fooled the Emperor. Now we have all the money we'll ever need."

And they ordered a sumptuous feast, including five roast chickens, six platters of pastries, gallons of wine and ten pink cupcakes with cherries on top.

Finally, they disappeared into their room to work. The Emperor hovered outside. He was longing to see his new clothes.

"Can't I just have a tiny peek?" he asked.

"No!" Slimus and Slick replied. "Nothing must disturb us. The slightest interruption could lead to a terrible mistake."

So the Emperor sent along his servant to take a look. His servant studied the looms. He couldn't see a thing, but he didn't want to seem foolish.

"Beautiful," he said. "The material is really, er, beautiful. The Emperor will be very impressed with your work. I'll go and let him know how well you're doing."

Isn't it super!

"You do that," said Slimus.

"And just remember," added Slick, "only VERY clever people can see our wonderful work."

"Oh yes," said the servant, nodding. He was thinking that he must be very foolish, and he had to make sure the Emperor never found out.

At last, the day dawned when the Emperor was allowed to see his new clothes. He raced up the palace steps and galloped along the corridors, brimming with glee. "So exciting!" he cried, a spring in his stride.

But when he arrived, he was stunned. "I can't see anything!" he thought to himself. "Yet my servant can... I must be very, very foolish. No one must ever find out."

So, out loud, he said, "Splendid! Amazing!

What wonderful clothes you have made, Slimus
and Slick. I can't wait to wear them."

"Thank you, Your Majesty," said Slimus.

"We knew you'd appreciate our work," added
Slimus, smiling.

The Emperor gave them each a gold medal for their work and even more money.

"Now," said Slick, stuffing the money into his pockets, then rubbing his hands with glee. "You must let us dress you for the Royal Procession."

"After all," said Slimus, "you want to look your best, don't you?"

"Here's your shirt," Slick went on. "Feel that material. It's light as gossamer, isn't it? You'll hardly notice you're wearing it at all."

The Emperor stared, and gulped. "Oh dear," he thought. He *still* couldn't see anything. But he just nodded and said, "Splendid!"

You'll look so grand!

"And now for the bottoms," said Slimus.

"And your cloak," said Slick. "This will be the finest outfit you've ever worn."

The Emperor's servant didn't know what to do. The Emperor looked really, well, really... NAKED.

As for the Emperor, he was getting so carried away by it all, he was almost sure he *could* see the clothes. "Aren't I handsome?" he crowed.

"You're ready at last," declared Slimus. "It's time for you to go to your Royal Procession. We're sure it's going to be one to remember."

The Emperor called in his footmen. "Don't I look fine?" he said.

The footmen gawped. "Yes, erm, very, erm, fine," they said. They were thinking they had never seen so much of the royal bottom before, but they didn't want to look foolish either, so they said absolutely nothing.

"Right!" the Emperor said to his servant. "Let the procession begin."

"Yes, Your Majesty," said his servant, looking straight up at the ceiling. "Not feeling at all chilly, are you? Would you like a coat perhaps?"

"Don't be ridiculous," snapped the Emperor.

75

The crowd gasped
when the Emperor appeared.
Everyone had heard that only clever people could
see his clothes.

"Amazing!" they cried. "Magnificent! Splendid!"

"Please can I see?" asked a small boy, who was stuck at the back of the crowd.

So his father lifted him up onto his shoulders. The boy pointed to the Emperor and cried out...

"He's naked!"

"He's right!" said his dad. "The Emperor *is* naked." The crowd began to laugh.

"Naked! Naked! Naked!" they chanted.
The Emperor blushed bright red. *All* over.

By now, Slimus
and Slick were
busy celebrating,
far, far away.

As for the Emperor, he shivered but he held his
head high. "After all," he said, "I am the Emperor
and the procession must go on!"

GOLDILOCKS AND THE THREE BEARS

There was once a little girl who lived in a snug cottage surrounded by wild flowers, tucked on the edge of a deep, dark forest.

The little girl's name was Goldilocks.

Goldilocks had long curly hair, as bright as the sun, and big round eyes as blue as the sky. Her cheeks flushed like pink rosebuds as she skipped through the meadows.

In fact, she looked like the sweetest, quietest, best-behaved girl you could ever meet. But oh dear...

...Goldilocks was the *naughtiest* little girl for miles around.

Yowl!

When her mother asked her to water the plants, poor Pickles the cat got an unexpected shower.

And when her father asked Goldilocks to paint the fence, she gave Digby the dog a coat of red roses.

Hee hee!

zzz

No matter how many times her parents pleaded, Goldilocks just couldn't seem to do as she was told.

One morning, her mother asked her to go to the village to buy a loaf of bread. "And make sure you keep to the path!" she called out.

But Goldilocks had only been gone a few
minutes, when she wandered from the path.
Soon she was in the heart of the
deep, dark forest.

Up ahead stood a
little thatched cottage.

"I wonder who lives there?"
thought Goldilocks.

Forgetting all about her errand,
she trotted down a hill and up to
the front door.

As she pushed open
the cottage door, a
sweet aroma came
wafting out.

"Mmmmm," thought
Goldilocks, sniffing the
air. "Something smells
really good."

There on a table were
three bowls of thick,
creamy porridge.

"Time for breakfast!"
said Goldilocks, licking
her lips.

Being a greedy little
girl, Goldilocks started
with the biggest bowl.
She stuck in a
spoon and swallowed
a great big mouthful...

Oww!

In a flash,
her cheeks turned
from pale pink to
bright red.
"Too hot!" she
gasped, dropping
the spoon in shock.

Goldilocks dashed to the kitchen and glugged down some water. It took three whole glasses before her mouth cooled down.

But Goldilocks was still hungry.

"Ah well," she thought, "perhaps the porridge in that middle-sized bowl won't be quite so hot."

Taking a slightly
smaller spoonful this
time, she popped the
porridge into her mouth.
The good news was that
it wasn't too hot...

"Bleurgh!" cried
Goldilocks with a
shiver. "Too cold!"
She threw down the
spoon in disgust and
set her sights on the
smallest bowl.

"This had better be good," she thought.

She sniffed the porridge cautiously. It certainly smelled good. Then she took a teeny tiny spoonful...

"Mmmm, just right."

Now she was sure the porridge was just how she liked it, Goldilocks gobbled it down in seconds.

"Aah, that was super yummy!" she said, with a little burp. She giggled.

"Time for a rest," sighed Goldilocks.

In front of the fireplace were three chairs. She threw herself onto the biggest one.

"Ow!" she yelled. "Too hard!"

Goldilocks jumped down, rubbing her sore bottom. "That must be the most uncomfortable chair in the world."

"This middle-sized one looks much more comfy," she thought.

It was padded all over and had two huge, plump cushions. Goldilocks jumped up onto the seat.

"Oof!" she yelped. "Too soft!"

Her legs and arms waggling in the air, she found herself swallowed up by the squashy cushions.

After several tries, she eventually gave up.

"Whew!" puffed Goldilocks. "Now I really *do* need to sit down. This small chair looks safe enough."

Aaaaah!

Goldilocks gingerly lowered herself onto the tiny little seat.

"Not too hard..." she said cautiously, "...and not too soft."

In fact, this chair was just right.

Now that she was certain that this chair was the best, Goldilocks bumped up and down in delight. It wasn't long before there came a loud 'Crack!' The tiny chair had broken into even tinier pieces.

Whooops!

Goldilocks looked down at the wreckage. "Oh well," she said. "It must have been really badly made. *Now* where can I relax?"

"I'll try upstairs," she thought. "There's bound to be a bed up there."

Yawning loudly, she made her way up the staircase.

Goldilocks had long forgotten the loaf of bread she was supposed to be buying. All she was interested in was a nice, long nap.

She opened a door and found herself in a big, bright bedroom with three different-sized beds.

"That biggest one has plenty of space to sprawl around," thought Goldilocks.

She tried to climb up, but it wasn't easy.

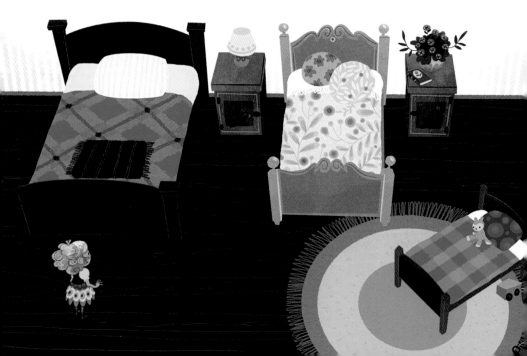

The thick mattress was way above her head. When she finally got on top, she wanted to come straight down.

"Too high!" she panted, dizzily.

She slid off carefully and padded over to the middle-sized bed.

"This is more my height," said Goldilocks, diving aboard.

"Help!" she cried, as she disappeared beneath a mass of squishy cushions and sank into the mattress. "Too deep! I'm drowning."

Goldilocks wiggled and wrestled. She got caught up in the blankets and tangled in the sheets.

At last, she tumbled onto the carpet.

Goldilocks was tired out. The only bed left to try was the smallest one.

"Hmmm... it feels okay," said Goldilocks.

It wasn't too high and it wasn't too deep. In fact, it was just right.

Goldilocks snuggled under the covers and tugged them up tightly around her. In no time at all, she was fast asleep.

A few minutes later, the owners of the little cottage returned from their morning walk.

They soon got a shock when they saw the mess on their breakfast table.

"Someone's been eating my porridge," growled Father Bear crossly.

"Someone's been eating *my* porridge," cried Mother Bear nervously.

"Someone's been eating *my* porridge," sniffed Baby Bear sadly, "and they've gobbled it *all* up."

But that was just the start...

"Look, someone's been sitting in my chair," grizzled Father Bear.

"Someone's been sitting in *my* chair," sighed Mother Bear.

"Someone's been sitting in *my* chair," cried Baby Bear, "and what's more, they've *broken* it!"

They stomped upstairs. "Someone's been sleeping in my bed," snorted Father Bear.

"Someone's been
sleeping in *my* bed,"
whined Mother Bear.

"Someone's been
sleeping in *my* bed,"
yelped Baby Bear,
"and she's *still in it!*"

Goldilocks woke
with a start to see
three very grumpy
bears staring right
at her.

"HELP!" she
screamed.

Goldilocks threw off the bedclothes, jumped out of bed, hurtled downstairs and shot out of the cottage. She ran and ran, faster than she'd ever run before, until she was safely home.

"I'm sorry I didn't get the bread," she puffed, hugging her mother tightly. "But I promise to do as I'm told from now on."

And do you know, from that day, Goldilocks kept her promise to be good.

Well, most of the time...

RUMPELSTILTSKIN

Once upon a time there was a miller who had a beautiful daughter. Her long fair hair was golden as the sun and she was the apple of her father's eye. He would talk of her all day long.

"She is the fairest maiden in the land," he boasted. "Her voice is more beautiful than a nightingale. She can dance like an angel and spin straw into gold."

"Spin straw into gold?" said his friends.

"Oh yes," said the miller.

Now, it just so happened that the King was passing through the village, and he overheard the miller's words.

"Your daughter can spin straw into gold?" he said. "Then bring her to me."

The miller beamed with pride and fetched his daughter.

Here she is, Your Majesty.

"Bring her to my castle," commanded the King, and galloped away.

The miller and his daughter followed on foot, with the miller's daughter dreaming of becoming Queen. "I'll dress in white velvet..." she thought.

"...and wear a golden crown upon my head."

But when they finally reached the castle, her dreams were shattered. The castle walls were cracked and crumbling. The wind whistled through its empty windows and the King stood on the overgrown path, watching her with a frown.

The King led the miller's daughter up a dark and twisting turret. "I have a challenge for you," he said. "If you complete it, you can be my wife. But if you fail... you'll lose your life."

"What is the challenge?" gasped the miller's daughter.

"I want you to spin this straw into gold," said the King. "Your father says you can do it...

...Now prove that it's true. You have until tomorrow morning," he told her. Then he went out of the room and locked the door.

The miller's daughter sat down and wept.
"I can't spin straw into gold," she sobbed. "Oh,
Father! Why did you make that foolish boast?"

Then, through the sound of her tears, she heard
a faint tapping at the window.

Outside, was a little man on a flying spoon.
"Let me in!" he cried. "Let me in! It's cold
out here on this frosty night."

"I can help you," he
promised. "But only if you
give me something in return."

"My necklace!" said the miller's daughter. "You can have my necklace?"

"It's a deal," said the little man. And he jumped from his spoon and bowed 'til his beard swept the floor. "At your service," he cackled.

Then he sat down
and began to spin.
"You can do it!"
cried the miller's
daughter. "You
really can."

Before her eyes, the little man spun straw into
gold. He worked all night, while the
miller's daughter slept and
smiled and dreamed.

In the morning, the little man was
gone but the room was lined with gold.

Gold
everywhere!

It sparkled. It glowed. It shone.
"Magic!" thought the miller's daughter.
"The little man must be magic. I'm saved.
Surely the King will be happy now?"

This way!

But the King took the miller's daughter by
the hand and led her further up the dark and
twisting turret. This time, the room was bigger
than the one before, and it was piled high with
bales of straw.

"Once again, you must spin this straw into gold.
If you fail, you'll lose your life...

118

...If you succeed, you can be
my wife." Then he went out and
locked the door.

Once again, the miller's daughter sat down
and wept. She prayed for the little man to come.
Outside, the owls hooted and the foxes barked.
"Please come, little man," whispered the miller's
daughter. "Please come."

At last, there was a tap at the window.

"What will you give me in return for my work?" asked the little man.

"This ring," said the miller's daughter.

So he stepped inside and began to spin.

In the morning, the room was
bursting with reels of gold.

"You've done it!" cried the King.
He was overjoyed.

"Just one more task," he said, leading the miller's daughter to a room far bigger than the one before. "Spin this straw into gold and tomorrow you shall be my wife. Otherwise, you'll lose your life."

Whirr, whirr...

That night, there came a tap at the window. But the miller's daughter had nothing left to give.

"I have an idea," said the little man. "I'll spin this straw to gold. But, in return, you must promise me your first-born child."

"I promise," said the miller's daughter. "Anything, so long as you save my life."

The next morning, the King rejoiced. The room was piled high with gold.

"More gold than I shall ever need," he said. "My crumbling castle can be restored. I'll fill it with furniture, drapes and jewels. And in return for such wealth, I'll make you my wife."

The King and the miller's daughter were married the next day. The crowds cheered loud and long for their new Queen, who had already forgotten about the little man and the promise she had so rashly made...

A year went by, and the Queen gave birth to
a baby girl, whom she loved more than life itself.

One wintry eve, she heard a tapping at her
window. The little man was back to claim his prize.

"That baby is mine," he said. "You promised her
to me in return for spinning straw into gold. Now
hand her over!"

"Never!" wept the Queen.

For a moment the little man relented. "You can keep your child," he said, "but only if you can guess my name. I'll give you three chances; that is all."

My baby!

All day, the Queen thought of the names she knew... but how could she tell which one belonged to the little man? When the King returned that evening, she could hardly eat or drink, until she heard his tale...

"On my way back from hunting," the King was saying, "I saw the strangest thing. A little man, in the middle of a forest, dancing around a fire.

And as he danced, he sang:

"Today I'll bake, tomorrow brew;
The next I'll do the same.
Ha! Glad I am that no one knew
That Rumpelstiltskin is my name!"

The Queen smiled but said nothing.

When the little man tapped on her window that night, she was ready for him.

"Is your name Mordechai?" she asked.

"No!" crowed the little man.

"It is Ezeka?"

"No!" cackled the little man.

"Then could it be... could it possibly be... RUMPELSTILTSKIN?"

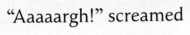

"Aaaaargh!" screamed
Rumpelstiltskin. And in
his fury...

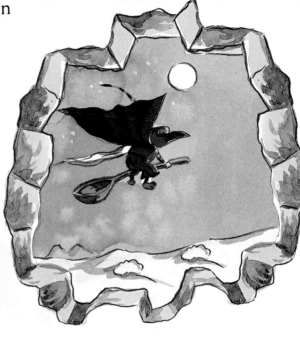

...he shot through the
wall, and was never,
ever seen again.

THE RELUCTANT DRAGON

Long ago, there was a peaceful little village called Sheepdale. But, one morning, its peace was shattered by the yells of a terrified shepherd.

"Heeeeellllllpp!" he hollered.

"Whatever's the matter?" cried his wife.

"S-s-something terrible!" he wailed. "As b-big as four horses, with l-long sharp claws, sh-shiny blue scales and a sp-spiky tail!"

The shepherd's son looked up from his book of myths and legends. "It sounds like a dragon to me," he said.

A dragon?

Yes, a dragon.

That night, the shepherd was too scared to sleep. And the next day, he didn't dare go into the hills to see his sheep.

"Don't worry, I'll go," said the boy.

"But what about the dragon?" his mother whispered.

The boy gave a shrug. "He might be friendly!" And off he skipped, up the hillside.

See you soon!

It wasn't hard to
find the dragon. He
was sitting outside a
cave, reciting poetry.

"Excuse me, young
sir," the dragon called.
"What rhymes
with beauty?"

"Er, duty?" replied the boy.

"Yes, that's it! Much better than fruity."

Not only was the dragon a poet, he was also a great storyteller and a vegetarian.

"In days gone by, dragons were fearsome fire-breathers," he told the boy, "burning down houses and stealing princesses. Ethelscorcher the Red was one of the most feared dragons of all…"

The boy loved hearing the dragon's stories and came back every day to listen.

But when the villagers found out about the dragon, they were terrified. "We must slay him before he slays us!" they cried.

The boy ran straight to the
dragon's cave. "The villagers
want to get rid of you!" he
panted. "You're not safe here."

They don't like
dragons.

"But I wouldn't hurt a fly," the dragon replied.
"Try telling that to the villagers," said the boy.
"But this is my home!"
"I know," sighed the boy. "But they want you out."
"I could read them some of my poetry?"

Back in the village, the mood had turned from fear to excitement.

"He's here!" cried the blacksmith.

"Who's here?" asked the boy.

"Saint George the Dragon Killer!"

A cheer came up from the crowd. "We're saved!"

He's going to fight the dragon!

Once more, the boy rushed to the dragon's cave. "Saint George has come to fight you!" he said. "And he's got the longest spear I've ever seen!"

"I don't like fighting," replied the dragon. "I'll hide in my cave until he goes away."

"You can't!" said the boy. "He's sure to find you here."

But the dragon just yawned and closed his eyes.

"There must be something I can do," thought the boy.

By now, the villagers had gathered around Saint George and were telling him fibs about the dragon.

"He eats ten sheep for breakfast!"

"He's burned down five houses already!"

The boy waited for the villagers to go. Then...

"It's not true!" he cried. "The dragon's my friend. He wouldn't hurt a fly."

Saint George scratched his chin. "How can you be so sure?" he asked.

"He recites poetry and he's a vegetarian. Does that sound fearsome to you?"

Saint George could see the boy had a point. "But I'm Saint George the Dragon Killer," he explained. "Everyone *expects* me to fight the dragon. I can't just go home."

"Wait a minute, that's it!" cried the boy. "We'll *stage* a great fight and then everyone will be happy. Quick! Let's go and tell the dragon."

The boy led George to the dragon's cave.
"What a perfect place for a fight!" said George.
Then the dragon appeared, looking very
grumpy. "Go away," he said. "I don't like fighting."

It will be fun!

"It doesn't have to be a real fight," said the boy, quickly. "You just need to put on a good show for the villagers."

"So there won't be any violence?" asked the dragon warily.

"Well it has to look real," said George.

"But you'll just be acting out a story," the boy assured him.

"I'm rather good at storytelling," said the dragon, warming to the idea.

It was Saint George's description of the feast they'd have after that finally convinced him.

On the day of the fight, the villagers were up
bright and early. They cheered and waved
when Saint George rode into view.
But where was the dragon?

Suddenly, a roar echoed around the hills and flames burst into view. Even the boy was taken by surprise.

Everyone gasped as the dragon emerged, his scales sparkling in the morning light, his breath threatening to burn anything in sight.

"Charge!" cried George, heading straight for the
dragon. He galloped hard, his spear held high.

The dragon bounded up to
meet him...

...and they shot
past each other.

"Missed!" yelled
the crowd.

George and the dragon turned around and charged again. This time there was no way they could miss. CLATTER! BANG! OUF!

The villagers covered their eyes and then peeked through their fingers. *Who was winning?* they wondered.

Finally, the dust settled and there was Saint George, standing victorious, the dragon slumped at his feet.

"Hurrah!" cheered the crowd.

"Cut off his head!" cried the blacksmith.

"I don't think that's necessary," said Saint George. "I think this brave and handsome dragon has learned his lesson. Let's invite him to join our feast." And George led the villagers, the boy and the dragon back down the hill.

That was awesome!

That evening, in the quiet
village of Sheepdale, there was the
loudest, most joyful party that
anyone could remember.

The boy was happy because his plan had
worked. The villagers were happy because they'd
seen a fight. George was happy because he'd won.
The dragon was happiest of all. He'd been the star
of the show, and now he had a very full tummy.

RAPUNZEL

Once upon a time there was a young woman
who had always longed for a baby, and now
she was finally going to have one. But oh! It made
her so hungry. And she wanted the strangest food –
in particular, the rapunzel that grew in the garden
beneath her window.

There was just one problem... The garden belonged to a witch!

"Please go and get me some rapunzel," she begged her husband.

"But the witch..." he protested. "What will she do to me?"

I'll die if I don't have it!

That night, under cover of darkness, the man crept into the witch's garden. He dashed from one flowerbed to the next. "Which is it?" he muttered. "Which is the rapunzel?"

This is terrifying!

When he got home, his wife was furious. "That's not rapunzel, you fool! It's a turnip! I don't want a turnip! You're going to have to go back."

"But I can't," said the man. "The witch!"

You have to!
Or else...

"Fine! I'll go," said the man, even though he trembled at the thought.

Once again, he waited until dark, then crept into the witch's garden in search of rapunzel.

No sooner had he plucked the pretty herb
from the ground than he heard a sharp cackle.
He looked up.

"Stealing from my garden, are you?" said
the witch.

"No, no," muttered the man. "It's for my wife, she's having a baby..."

"Oh, a baby! I see! Well, you can take the rapunzel now you've picked it, but you'll have to pay. That baby is mine. I'll come and get it as soon as it's born!"

Terrified, the man agreed.

The witch kept her word. No sooner had the baby been born, than she stormed into their house. "A girl," she said, gazing at the baby. "I'll call her Rapunzel."

Mine!

"Don't take her!" cried the mother. "I'll do anything, *anything*!"

"Please," begged the father.

But the witch only laughed. "Too late," she said. And she whisked the baby to her house, deep in the woods.

As soon as she was old enough, Rapunzel
had to work for the witch, day and night. She
collected slugs and snails for her spells, cooked
and cleaned...

Fetch me some frogs!

...and longed for a different home. But there was
no escape. The witch always watched her with
a beady eye. As Rapunzel grew into a beautiful
young girl, she watched her more carefully still.

On Rapunzel's sixteenth birthday, the witch looked out at her in the garden and thought, "She's grown too pretty. There's nothing else to do! I'm going to have to lock her up!"

The witch took Rapunzel to a tower in the middle of the forest. Then, with a snap of her fingers and a the chant of a spell, she cast Rapunzel into the topmost room of the tower. There was no way out – no stairs and no doors. Rapunzel was trapped.

All day, Rapunzel would gaze out of her window, with only the birds for company.

She wished she had wings too, so she could fly to freedom.

Whenever the witch came with food and water, she would cry, "Rapunzel, Rapunzel! Let down your golden hair!"

And Rapunzel would let down her long locks so they tumbled like a waterfall to the ground far below.

Then the witch would seize the hair in her hands and start to climb.

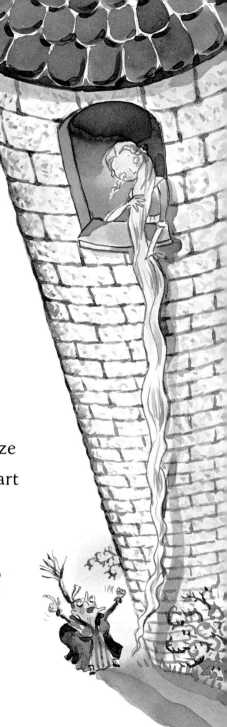

Rapunzel, Rapunzel!

Her old bones
creaking, and her
voice groaning, the
witch heaved herself
up the side of the
tower and into
Rapunzel's room.

"Will you ever let me go?" Rapunzel would ask.
"Never!" the witch would reply.

Where am I?

Then, one day, a handsome Prince found his way into the forest. He spied Rapunzel's beautiful face, gazing out from the tower. A moment later, he saw the witch approach and hid from view. He watched and he waited...

As soon as the witch had gone, the
Prince emerged from his hiding place and
called out, "Rapunzel, Rapunzel! Let
down your golden hair."

Then he carefully took hold of the
golden locks and began to climb.

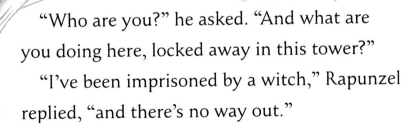

"Who are you?" he asked. "And what are
you doing here, locked away in this tower?"

"I've been imprisoned by a witch," Rapunzel
replied, "and there's no way out."

"You could cut off your hair," said the Prince. "Then we could climb down it together."

"No!" cried Rapunzel, hugging her golden locks. "I have a better idea. Visit me every evening, for the witch comes by day, and each time you visit, bring a strand of silk. I'll weave it into a ladder."

Every evening after that, the Prince came to visit Rapunzel in her tower. They would talk of everything and nothing, and all the time her ladder grew longer and longer. One evening, Rapunzel even promised that when she left the tower, she would become the Prince's wife.

"You'll love my palace," said the Prince. "It has tall turrets that touch the sky. There are servants who will wait on you hand and foot, and beautiful gardens bursting with roses. As soon as you are free, I will take you there."

Rapunzel longed for that day.

She dreamed of the palace and her new life.

Only one more rung and I'll be free.

But one day, as the witch climbed up the tower, Rapzunzel said, "How is it that you are so much heavier than the Prince?"

"What's this?" shrieked the witch. "You've betrayed me!" And she hacked off Rapunzel's hair.

With a powerful spell, she cast Rapunzel into the wilderness. Then she waited for the Prince to come.

"Rapunzel, Rapunzel!" he called that night. "Let down your golden hair."

Little did he know that this time it was the witch who let down Rapunzel's hair.

Ha ha! It is I!

As the Prince reached the window, the wicked witch kissed his hands. Instantly, they were covered in thick slime. The Prince tried to hold on but his fingers slipped... He lost his grip and fell down, down, landing in brambles, where the thorns scratched at his eyes.

Blinded, he stumbled up again, crying, "Rapunzel! I'll find you somehow!"

For many years, the Prince searched the world for Rapunzel. At last he heard tell of a beautiful woman with golden hair, who lived in the wilderness. He rushed to find her, his heart full of hope.

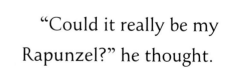

"Could it really be my Rapunzel?" he thought.

And it was. She ran to him and hugged him and as her tears fell on the Prince's eyes, he was no longer blinded.

"After all these years, I have found you," he said. "Now come to my palace and be my wife."

Rapunzel and the Prince were soon married. Everyone was invited to the wedding – everyone, that is, except the witch.

And of all the people at the wedding, two were especially overjoyed to see Rapunzel.

A man and a woman ran to her, saying, "We think you must be our daughter, stolen by the witch so long ago."

"My parents!" cried Rapunzel. And from that moment on, Rapunzel and her Prince lived happily ever after.

TOM THUMB

Once upon a time, a farmer named Thomas lived with his dear wife Eve. They had everything they could wish for – except for a child.

"Even one the size of my thumb would do," said Thomas with a sad smile.

Eve decided to ask Merlin the Magician. She
ventured into the ancient forest to find him.

"So you want a child, do you?" spoke Merlin.

"Oh yes please," said Eve. "Even one the size of
a thumb would do."

Merlin chuckled and raised his right hand.
"Abracadoo! Then your wish shall come true."

Eve rushed home to tell Thomas the good news. They swept their cottage, painted the walls and hoped with all their hearts.

Sure enough, before the end of the year, Eve gave birth to a teeny, tiny baby boy. He was so small, she could hold him in the palm of her hand.

"Our very own son," said Thomas proudly.

"He's perfect," said Eve. "What shall we call him?"

"That's easy," Thomas replied.

Tom Thumb!

Eve made their little son his own clothes to wear.

His top was stitched
in the finest cobweb
strands.

His bottoms were
knitted from soft
lamb's wool.

His pointy shoes were
cobbled together from
shiny apple skin.

And Thomas found
him a hat to match – a
little, furled-up oak leaf.

Tom Thumb grew older and stronger. He learned to walk and talk and run and jump...

...but he barely grew any bigger.

"It will be hard being small," Eve told her son.

"Don't worry," Tom replied. "I'll be fine."

One morning, Eve made some buns to sell at the market. Little Tom loved helping in the kitchen.

When it was time to go, Eve couldn't find Tom anywhere, so she headed off to the market alone.

A hungry customer bought a bun, broke it open...

Surprise!

...and got the shock of his life. Poor Eve didn't know whether to laugh or cry.

"Don't worry," said Tom. "I'm fine."

The next day Eve took Tom to milk the cows.
"Now stay there where I can see you," she said,
perching him on a thistle flower.

Unfortunately, cows like thistles.

One moment Tom was sitting happily by a cow. The next moment he'd disappeared.

"Tom!" shrieked Eve. She searched the grass in a panic. Just then, the cow let out a burp...

...and Tom tumbled from its mouth.

Poor Eve didn't know whether to laugh or cry.

"Don't worry," said Tom. "I'm fine!"

A week later, Tom went to sow seeds with his
father. Thomas taught his little son how to stand
up and be a scarecrow.

Unfortunately, the crows weren't at all scared of Tom Thumb. In fact, one of the crows swooped down and carried him away.

"Let me go!" cried little Tom.

And the crow did just that. Down and down Tom fell, until he landed SPLASH! in the lake below.

As Tom tried to swim to safety, a greedy fish glided up to meet him. Its fins were moving fast and its mouth was opened wide.

First, the fish swallowed Tom, then it swallowed a fisherman's hook.

"Got you!" cried the fisherman, reeling in his catch.

That evening, at the royal castle, King Arthur sat down to his evening meal.

"It's fresh fish today sir," announced a squire.

Delicious!

King Arthur was about to take a bite when he got the shock of his life.

"Surprise!" cried Tom Thumb.

King Arthur liked Tom Thumb from the start.

"I'm an excellent juggler," said Tom, as he scattered peas all over the table.

Merlin and the knights of the round table liked
Tom Thumb too.

"I can kill a fly with one poke of my needle,"
Tom said bravely.

"Then I shall make you a knight," announced
the King. "You shall have a gallant white mouse for
a horse and a twig for a lance."

Bravo Tom!

Hurrah!

And that's how little Tom Thumb became *Sir*
Tom, the smallest knight in the kingdom.

Tom charged fearlessly into battle against
threatening insects. He hunted down spiders and
chased after dragonflies.

You can't
catch me!

When he wasn't
fighting foes, he was
collecting fallen petals
for the Queen or saving
moths from drowning
in the castle moat.

"Your Majesty,"
said Tom one day.
"I think I should
visit my parents."
    "Why of course,"
said the kind King.
"Take them a gold
coin from me."

Tom bid farewell to his castle friends.
"Take care, little knight," the Queen said,
fondly. "It's a big world out there."

"Don't worry," said Tom. "I'll be fine." And he rode off on his gallant white mouse.

Tom!

Woof!

Tom's journey didn't exactly
go smoothly. There were ants to
avoid, vast puddles to cross and
terrifying raindrops to dodge. But
Tom was a brave knight, sent by the
King, with an important coin to deliver.

Finally he arrived home to his delighted parents.
Poor Eve didn't know whether to laugh or cry.

"Is it really you?" asked Thomas.

"Yes it's me," said Tom. "Although I'm *Sir* Tom
now and I've brought you a gift from King Arthur."

Tom's parents listened in amazement as he described his adventures. He told them tales of crows and fishes, pea juggling and petal collecting, spider hunting and moth rescuing.

"Who would have thought our son would become the smallest knight in the kingdom!" said Thomas proudly.

"I like being the size of a thumb," said Tom.

A week later, Sir Tom was ready for his next adventure. Eve and Thomas were sad to see him go, but they knew they couldn't stop him.

"Come back soon," said Thomas.
"Take care, little Tom," said Eve.
"It's a big world out there."

"Don't worry," said Tom. "I'll be fine." And he rode off once more, on his gallant white mouse.

Goodbye!

THE GOOSE GIRL

Once there was a beautiful Princess named Rose. She lived in a grand house with every luxury you could imagine. But Rose wasn't snooty. In fact, she was the sweetest princess for miles around.

One day, Rose was walking in the palace gardens with her mother, when the Queen turned to her with a smile.

"It's time you were married, Rose," she said. "The Prince of Pavlova has heard all about you, and would like you to pay him a visit."

Rose couldn't wait to meet the Prince. She'd heard he was not only kind, but handsome too.

"I'm hosting a royal garden party, so I shall have
to stay here," said the Queen, "but your maid
Grizelda can go with you. I'll be thinking of you,
though," added the Queen. Then she handed Rose
a golden necklace. "This is a little gift from me for
the journey."

On the necklace hung a golden locket that glittered and glinted in the flickering candlelight.

"Thank you, Mother," said Rose, "It's lovely."

"It *is* rather special," said the Queen with a smile.

I can see all that you do.

It sings!

I will be a friend to you.

"Promise you won't lose it," added the Queen.

"Of course," replied Rose. Her parents had brought her up never to break a promise, and she never had.

The next morning, Rose and Grizelda set off on their journey. From the moment the grumpy maid climbed on her horse, she was cruel to it.

Rose, on the other hand, had nothing but kind words for her horse, Falada. She stroked his mane gently and whispered softly in his ear.

"I'm not too heavy for you, I hope?" she asked.

"Not at all, Princess," replied Falada. "But thank you for asking."

Rose was already starting to miss her mother. But the locket around her neck reminded her that the Queen was thinking of her.

Good boy.

I do my best.

The sun was high
in the sky when they reached
a sparkling stream.

"Why don't you take my
cup from the saddle bag," Rose
suggested to her maid. "Then we can
both have a cooling drink."

"What a good idea," replied Grizelda with a
sneaky grin.

She took the cup from the bag, barged past Rose
and ran down to the water's edge.

The greedy maid gulped down mouthful after mouthful. Then she let the cup fall into the rushing river. "Oops, butter fingers!" she cried.

Now Rose had to lie on the hard ground to scoop up the water in her hands.

♪ If your mother only knew, ♪ it would break her heart in two.

As Rose stood up, the dainty chain of the locket snagged on a nearby branch.

Snap! went the chain, and the precious present fell into the swirling water.

"Oh no!" wailed Rose. "My beautiful locket, lost forever."

"Ha ha!" laughed Grizelda. "What will the
Queen say when she finds out you've lost the
locket she gave you?"

"Oh please don't tell her," sighed Rose.
"I gave her my word I wouldn't lose it.
And I never break a promise."

Don't be mean, Grizelda!

Hee hee!

"Well," said Grizelda, "I won't tell on you, but only if you do something for me."

"All right," said Rose, "anything you want."

Grizelda gazed admiringly at the Princess's beautiful gown.

"Let me exchange dresses with you," said the maid.

"Um, very well then," agreed Rose, slightly puzzled.

Once they'd changed, Grizelda threw herself onto Falada's back.

"I'll take your clever horse too," she cried.

Ouch!

"Now promise you won't tell a living thing we traded places," added Grizelda.

"I promise," sighed Rose, as they trotted on with their journey.

When at last they reached the palace at Pavlova, the Prince himself rushed out to greet them.

"You must be Princess Rose," he said to Grizelda.

"Er, that's right," lied the maid. She pointed to Rose, "And this is my servant, Grizelda."

"Welcome to Pavlova, Grizelda," said the King as he led everyone inside.

"You must be tired after your long journey," said the Prince to the phoney princess.

"It was boring too," snorted Grizelda, "with only my dull little maid for company."

Grizelda was glad to see that Falada had been taken far from the palace, where no one would hear him talk. She wanted Rose out of the way too. "Perhaps you can find a job for my maid?" she asked.

Rose was desperate to tell the Prince that
Grizelda wasn't really a princess. But she'd made
a promise and she couldn't break it.

The next day, Rose was given the job of helping
a boy named Conrad look after the royal geese.

On the way, they
passed Falada, tied
to a tree.

"Poor Falada,"
sighed Rose.

"Poor Princess,"
whinnied Falada.

Conrad was astounded.
He'd never heard a horse
talk before.

"Why did he call you
'Princess'?" he asked, as they
walked on to the meadow.

"I'm sorry, but I can't
tell you," replied
Rose with a wave
to her loyal horse.

When they reached the meadow, they sat in the long grass, while the geese pecked around. Rose took out a comb and brushed her long golden hair. Conrad had never seen such lovely locks before.

He tried to pull out a few strands for a keepsake. But Rose was too quick for him.

Smiling to herself,
she chanted a rhyme.
"Blow now, gentle
wind I say. Blow this
goose boy's hat away."

Conrad's hat somehow
flew off his head and fluttered
away across the fields. He had to chase it for miles.

When he finally caught it and returned to the
meadow, Rose had tied up her hair in a bun.

That evening, Conrad went to the King. "That goose girl is strange," he said, telling him all about his hat and Falada.

Poor princess.

The King was intrigued. The next day, he followed Conrad and Rose. He heard Rose and Falada talking...

...and he watched as Conrad grabbed at Rose's hair and his hat magically blew away.

Later, the King visited Rose in the kitchens,
as she helped prepare a special banquet.

"Are you really a *princess*?" he asked.

"I promised not to tell a living thing," replied
Rose sadly.

The King thought for a moment. "You could

always tell this
cupboard," he suggested.

Rose climbed inside
and told it all that had
happened.

The King frowned.

He took Rose
to the royal maids
and asked them to
give her a sweet-
smelling soapy
bubble bath....

...style her hair in the
latest fashion, with
long, curly ringlets...

...and dress her in the
most elegant, beautiful
gown with a puffed
skirt and fancy ribbons.

224

"It will be a pleasure to escort you to the banquet," said the King. He sat her alongside the Prince and whispered what had happened in his son's ear.

Just then, Grizelda strode into the dining hall. "Who's that sitting in my chair next to the Prince?" she bawled, not recognizing Rose. "Get out, or I'll have the King punish you!"

The King smiled and turned to Grizelda.

"Now tell me," he asked, "what punishment should I give to someone who was mean, selfish and told lies?"

Grizelda grinned. "Well, they should be made to live in a smelly old pigsty," she giggled, "up to their knees in gloopy mud."

"Good idea!" said the King. "So that's exactly what we'll do with you."

Grizelda was dragged from the palace and flung into the stinkiest pigsty on the palace farm.

"Help!" wailed the mean maid as she squelched down into the mud.

As for Rose, it wasn't long before she and the
Prince were married. The happy couple made a
promise to love each other forever more – and they
never broke it.

THE TINDER BOX

om the soldier couldn't wait to get home. He'd spent the past five years in the army, and he was looking forward to a well-earned rest from all the marching and boot-polishing.

As he strolled along, Tom heard a rustle from the nearby bushes and an old woman leaped out in front of him.

"How would you like to be really, really rich, soldier?" she cried with a wild grin.

"Well, who wouldn't?" replied Tom when he'd recovered from the shock.

The old woman pointed a bony finger at a gnarled, hollow tree. "Under there lies a cave full of treasure – and it's all yours."

"I just want an old
tinder box you'll find down
there," added the woman.
"I can't get it myself
because the cave is full
of fireflies and they
scare me to pieces."

You've got
a deal!

"The three
treasure chests are
guarded by fierce
dogs," warned
the woman. "But
lay them on this
apron and they
won't harm you."

Armed with the apron
and a length of rope from
his bag, Tom climbed to the
top of the hollow tree.

He tied one
end of his rope to
a branch and lowered
himself inside the trunk.

Down and down
he went. At first it
was pitch black. But
as he got lower, Tom
could make out a faint
light beneath him.
Gradually it became
brighter and brighter.

At last, Tom's feet touched solid ground and he found himself in an echoing cave, illuminated by the golden glow of hundreds of tiny fireflies.

Up ahead were three oak doors, each one carved with the head of a dog.

"The treasure chests must be in there," thought Tom nervously. Clutching the apron tightly, he tugged at the first door, which swung open with a creepy creak.

Tom gasped. A big,
growling dog, with eyes
as big as tea cups, was
perched on a crimson
treasure chest.

Tom unfurled the apron,
picked up the dog...

...and placed him
gently on top.

Then he eased
open the chest.

Hundreds of bright copper
coins cascaded onto the floor.
He scooped them up and put
the dog back on the chest.

I'm rich!

In the next room was an even bigger dog, with eyes as big as saucers. Tom took a deep breath and lugged the dog onto the apron.

When he opened the second chest, thousands of shiny silver coins streamed out.

I'm really rich!

The final room was the scariest of all. Slumped over a chest was a gigantic dog, with eyes as big as dinner plates.

It took all Tom's strength to heave him onto the apron.

When the last chest was opened, what seemed like a million glittering gold coins poured out.

I'm really, really rich!

Tom stuffed as many coins as he could into his bag and his hat. He was just about to leave, when he remembered the old woman's request. Sure enough, wedged between two stones was a little brass tinder box.

Tom added the box to his treasure and hauled himself up the rope. It was a lot harder than climbing down, but eventually he was back outside.

"Here's your tinder box," said Tom, plucking the tin from his bag. As he did so, a tiny firefly buzzed out and landed on the old woman's nose.

"Nooooo!" she cried out.

Kapoof!

There was a puff of smoke and the old woman vanished.

"That was no ordinary old lady," thought Tom. "I think she was a witch!"

Tom strode into the nearest town, his bag clinking and clunking with his new-found treasure. Until a few hours ago, he'd been a badly-paid soldier. Now he was super rich.

Tom headed for the swankiest hotel he could find. "A suite of your best rooms please," he said, tossing down a handful of gold coins.

For a while, Tom enjoyed fine living. He splashed out on tailor-made clothes and dined in the best restaurants. But he was also kind-hearted, and soon he had given away all his money to the poor.

In no time, Tom went from riches to rags. All he had left was the tinder box.

"I'll light this candle to keep warm," he said with a shiver.

I'm f..f..freezing!

He took a flintstone, a piece of steel and some cloth from the tinder box. He struck the steel with the flint to make sparks. But instead of setting light to the cloth so that Tom could light his candle, they swirled magically across the room.

What's going on?

From the shower of sparks, a huge dog appeared.

"It's a dog from the cave," gasped Tom in disbelief. "The one with eyes as big as tea cups."

"Your wish is my command, master," barked the dog. "What do you desire?"

Tom could hardly believe his ears. A talking dog? Offering wishes?

"Well, I could really use some money..." he began.

Without waiting, the dog
raced from the room, returning
moments later with a bulging bag
of coins. Tom sat
open-mouthed.

He soon found that two strikes with the flint
brought the second dog. Three strikes made the
third dog appear. And both dogs
could make his wishes come
true, just like the first one.

Now he knew
why the witch had
wanted the
tinder box. By
the end of the
night, Tom
was rich again.

Tom used his new wealth to buy a grand house in the middle of town and life was good.

He was having breakfast one morning, when he heard the sound of hooves on the cobbles outside.

"That'll be the King and Queen going for their weekly carriage ride," said Tom's maid, Meg.

Tom leaned out of the window to take a look.

"Why are there no cheering crowds?" asked Tom.

"No one likes that snooty pair," snorted Meg. "They keep the poor Princess locked in her room at the palace, and never let her go out. Didn't you know?"

"I've been away in the army a long time," explained Tom. He felt sorry for the Princess and was determined to meet her. "I think I have an idea..."

That night, he took out the tinder box and summoned the dog with eyes as big as tea cups.

"Please bring the Princess from the palace," he asked the faithful hound.

With a glint in his eye and a wag of his tail, the dog padded off into the night.

Minutes later, the dog returned with the sleeping Princess on his back. As soon as Tom set eyes on her, he fell hopelessly in love.

At first light, the dog gently took the Princess back to the palace.

When she awoke that morning, the Princess told her parents about a dream she'd had.

"I visited a handsome stranger," she said, yawning.

"Perhaps it wasn't just
a dream," the King
grumbled to his wife.

"We'll know if
it happens again,"
replied the Queen
with a sly grin.

That night, as soon as the Princess was asleep,
the Queen tied a bag of flour to her daughter's
nightdress. Then she
made a tiny hole in
the bag.

An hour later,
the dog carried
the Princess to
Tom's house
once again.

Early the following morning, the dog returned the Princess as before.

But as the sun rose, the King followed the telltale trail of flour from the palace to Tom's house.

"Got you!" the King roared at Tom. "No one sees the Princess and lives."

Tom was thrown into the deepest, darkest palace dungeon to await his fate.

"I'll never see the Princess again," he sighed.

As dawn approached, his maid Meg appeared.

"I just came to say goodbye, sir," she sniffed.

"Cheer up, Meg," said Tom. "I've had an idea. Please bring me my tinder box."

Meg followed Tom's instructions.

Moments after she'd handed him the tinder box, Tom was dragged from the dungeon and marched across the courtyard.

Everyone in the kingdom had heard what had happened and they all felt sorry for the soldier. People soon gathered to shout their support.

"Silence, peasants!" barked the King.

"Yes," agreed his wife, as she swished past. "Any more of that and you'll be next!"

"It's now or never," thought Tom, as he sneaked the tinder box from his pocket.

As quickly as he could, Tom struck the steel with the flint once... twice... three times.

In an instant, the three dogs bounded from a cloud of sparks.

"Chase this wicked King and Queen from the kingdom!" ordered Tom.

Howling and growling, the dogs obeyed.

Tom freed the Princess and soon after they were married. The kingdom had a new King and Queen and everyone was invited to the wedding party. Even the tinder box had its own special cushion, guarded by the three loyal dogs.

Edited by Lesley Sims
Cover and additional illustrations: Lorena Alvarez
Digital imaging: Nick Wakeford